# Snow Fight
## A Warcraft® Tale

Story by Chris Metzen

Art by Wei Wang

extra credit:

kat, micky, cate, michele, doug, justin, joshua, and special thanks to jerry and tak

First Blizzard Entertainment Hardcover Edition November 2013
Manufactured in Malaysia
10 9 8 7 6 5 4 3 2 1
ISBN 978-0-9897001-0-8

www.blizzard.com
www.worldofwarcraft.com

This book is dedicated to
Sofia and Lucas.
You are imagination.

- C M

This book is dedicated to my sons,
Jason and Vincent.
I enjoy every day with you.

- WW

ong ago, in the world of Azeroth...
It was a cold day, a snowy day,
when Varian and Thrall walked home.

"I **love** winter time!" said Varian excitedly.
"I love skating and building ice-forts –
and all the Winter Veil **goodies** we get!"

"I like winter, too," Thrall replied thoughtfully.
"It's like all of nature takes a **big long nap**
until the spring comes."

"I guess I never thought about it like *that...*"
said Varian.

"...but right now, all I care about is...

SNOWBALL FIGHTS!"

"Sounds fun to me!" Thrall replied.
"But you never know who else
is looking to pick a fight!"

Varian shrugged.

"I'm not worried! I've got the fastest
hardpacked snowball in the kingdom!"

# SSSHH!

Suddenly, a HUGE snowball
smashed Varian right in the face!

The two boys heard a cold voice holler,

"Tremble at my power!

I'm the Master of
Icy Awesomeness!"

here, standing on a lumpy throne of ice, was the neighborhood bully, **Arthas**.

"Go on home to mommy, Varian! You'll **never** beat me!" Arthas yelled.

"That mean ol' Arthas!" Varian said as
Thrall helped him up. "I wasn't even ready yet!
I'll show him who's KING around here!"

Thrall brushed the snow off his friend.

"It was just a lucky shot," Thrall told him.
"Maybe you should calm down before you make
this a REAL fight?"

"Y'know, you're a real blockhead, Arthas," Varian said.

"Whatever, Varian," Arthas snapped.

"I tagged you fair and square!"

"Only because I wasn't looking!

It's no wonder no one ever wants to play with YOU!"

**"OH YEAH?"** Arthas yelled.
And then with no warning,
Arthas PUSHED him off the throne!

"Okay, that's it!" Varian yelled angrily.

"That ol' Arthas is really going to get it!"

Thrall tried to calm his friend down.

"He's just being a big bully," he said.

"He WANTS to get you mad."

"Well I AM!" roared Varian.

Varian ran at the Frozen Throne
and KICKED IT with all his might!
"HEEE-YAH! he cried"

The lumpy, frosty throne
toppled right over!
Arthas tumbled with a yelp!

"What's the matter, Arthas?" Varian teased.

"YOU gonna cry now?"

Varian looked down at the miserable bully.

"How do YOU like it, huh?" he asked.

"Not so tough now, are ya?"

Arthas just sat quietly as the wet snow
dripped off his helmet.

Thrall stepped in between the two boys.

He was disappointed in his friend.

"Who's being the bully **now,** Varian?" he asked.
"Arthas was wrong to be mean, but you being
mean right back just makes it **worse!**"

All of a sudden, Varian felt bad.

He knew Thrall was right...

... he had been just as mean as Arthas.

Thrall helped Arthas stand up.

"You know, Arthas," Thrall said,
"if you were a little nicer, we'd be
happy to play with you."

"Really?" asked Arthas.

"Absolutely!" replied Thrall.

*"Rjiiiiight, Varian?"*

Arthas reached his hand out to Varian.

He NERVOUSLY cleared his throat and said,
"I know I've been a blockhead. I guess with all my
practicing to become an invincible overlord
of darkness, I sometimes treat people like
they're just dumb ol' minions or somethin'."

"I'll try to be nicer from now on, okay?"
Arthas said with a smile.

"Good enough for me!" Varian replied excitedly.

"Well, now that we're all friends..." said Varian.

"... What should we do with the rest of the day?"

A mischievous grin crept across Thrall's face.

"WELL..." he said slyly,
"we still have a snowball fight
to get back to!"

Thrall used his weather powers to
make the wind and snow SWIRL all around them.

"Uh oh..." said Varian.

"... I know what that means!"

# AFTERWORD

As many of you may have noticed, this book is a bit different from our standard Warcraft fare. And really, that was always the point of creating it.

After nine exciting years of adventuring through the lands of Azeroth—whether it was through playing the game itself or reading our expanded fiction based on Warcraft's legendary characters—we wanted to take a moment to stop and appreciate how much livin' in the "real world" we've all done during the game's run time.

Many of us who started playing *WoW* way back in 2004 have had some pretty amazing life events happen—not least of which was becoming parents ourselves and watching as our own kids grew curious about this thing we're into called *World of Warcraft* . . .

The reason we created this book was to find cool, fun ways of sharing some of Warcraft's characters and ideas with our kids. While the game's learning curve might be a bit too steep for a four- or five-year-old (uh . . . or a rusty forty-year-old, from time to time, ahem . . . ), telling lighter stories about the game's heroes and villains seemed like a perfect way to share our passion for Warcraft with the young, imaginative minds we love most.

So, while *Snow Fight* won't necessarily be setting any new fictional precedents for Warcraft's epic saga, we dearly hope it offers a fun, lighthearted opportunity to "get lost" with your own rug rats in a world of orcs and elves, heroes and villains, and endless imagination!

Chris Metzen
July 2013